First published in Great Britain in 2000 by Macdonald Young Books

Macdonald Young Books,
an imprint of Wayland Publishers Ltd
61 Western Road
Hove
East Sussex
BN3 1JD

Text © Pat Thomas 2000
Illustrations © Lesley Harker 2000
Volume © Macdonald Young Books 2000

Editor: Lisa Edwards
Series designer: Kate Buxton
Book designer: Jean Wheeler

A CIP catalogue for this book is available from the British Library

Printed and bound in Portugal by Edições ASA

ISBN 0 7500 2888 2

Find Macdonald Young Books on the Internet
at http://www.myb.co.uk

My Brother, My Sister and Me

A FIRST LOOK AT SIBLING RIVALRY

PAT THOMAS
ILLUSTRATED BY LESLEY HARKER

MACDONALD YOUNG BOOKS

Do you have a brother or sister?
Do you sometimes wish that
you didn't?

Do you ever imagine how nice it would be if you were the only child in your family?

Everyone who has a brother or
sister feels this way sometimes.

Especially when they follow you around without being asked or draw pictures in your favourite book.

What about you?

What do you think life would
be like if you didn't have
a brother or sister?

When you have a brother or sister
it may feel like you never
get the right sort
of attention.

Either you
don't get noticed
when you've done
something good or you
get noticed too often when
you do something naughty.

It can be hard to like your brother or sister when you think that your parents love them more or that they are better at everything than you are.

But everybody is special. Each person has things that they are good at and things they are bad at.

What about you?

Do you ever wish you were more like your brother or sister? What things are you good at?

When you're feeling unhappy about
having a brother or sister the last thing
you feel like doing is sharing with them.

But in families everybody
has to learn to share.

The bigger your family is, the more you will
have to learn to share things like toys, the
television and your parents' attention.

Sharing can be hard. But fighting is even harder. It is terrible to live in a house where children are always fighting and competing with each other.

Often parents don't know what to do to
make things peaceful again.

It is hard for them to be fair to each of you
every minute of every day.

Even though
having a brother
or sister can be hard
work, it can also be fun
because it means you can have
more of lots of good things.

After all, there is more
chance that someone
will be there to play
with you and teach
you new games.

When you have a brother or sister you
always have someone to share secrets with
or share chores with.

There are more people in the house
to love and take care of you.

When you have a nightmare, your brother or sister may be the first one there to chase the monsters away. At school, they may protect you from bullies.

What about you?

Do you enjoy sharing with your brother or sister?
What kinds of things do you do together?

All families need to learn how to get on with each other. Everyone, even parents, has to keep practising being fair and sharing with others.

You don't all have to be the same, look the same or like the same things to like each other. In fact, families can be a lot more interesting when everyone is allowed to be themselves.

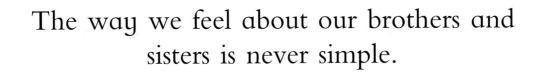

The way we feel about our brothers and
sisters is never simple.

Even when
you are grown up
it is sometimes hard
to understand how you
feel about them.

Some grown-ups still feel that they have to compete with their brothers and sisters.

This can make them very unhappy. That's why it's best to learn how to get on right from the start.

The important thing to remember is that even though you fight sometimes, it doesn't mean you have stopped loving each other.

And even though you, your brother and your sister may be very different, your parents love each of you.

HOW TO USE THIS BOOK

The way children feel about their brothers and sisters is very complex. Often they will feel a wide range of emotions long before they are able to say what those emotions are. Parents and teachers can help in many ways.

Here are some simple guidelines:

Try to avoid comparing one child with another. When you do this you lock your children into roles that they may never get out of (i.e. the good one, the naughty one). Instead it is important to respect the differences between your children and affirm that these differences are alright with you.

Sometimes even sensitive parents allow insensitive things to happen between their children. You can't always get it right so don't be too hard on yourself. Instead, focus on what you might do differently next time.

Parents can sometimes contribute to sibling rivalry. It is a family problem, not a problem which exists only between children. How you handle your children's arguing may reflect what you experienced in your own childhood. Make sure it reflects it in a positive way. If you are doing the same negative things to your children that your parents did to you, now is the time to break the pattern.

Teachers need to be aware of not making comparisons between siblings, but to encourage the individuality of each child at whatever stage of development. An eye-opening project about fantasies and expectations within families would be to have children with brothers and sisters write about what life would be like without their siblings and have only-children write about what life would be like with a sibling. Answers could be compared in class and used to promote lively discussion.

Try to get past the idea that your children should be great friends. Friendship is based on similarities. Sibling relationships, by their very nature, are based on differences. A better goal is to help your children develop the skills to get on with other people, to learn to respect differences, resolve difficulties and make a caring relationship. These skills will support them through the whole of their lives.

Alternatively, for older children, a family-tree exercise is useful to help children see that nobody is perfect and each of us is different. Children can be encouraged to list the best and worst qualities of everyone in the family (including themselves).

BOOKS TO READ

For Adults

Siblings Without Rivalry
How to help your children live together so you can live too
by Adele Faber and Elaine Mazlish
(Avon, 1988)

For Children

It's Mine
by Ewa Lipniacka and Basia Bogdanowicz
(Mage Publications, 1992)

It's Not Fair
by Brian Moses and Mike Gordon
(Wayland Publishers, 1997)

The Second Princess
by Tony Ross
(Anderson Press, 1994)

USEFUL CONTACTS

The Parent's Network
44-46 Caversham Road
London NW5 2DS
0171-485-8535
*Runs "parent-link" groups which offer
a listening ear and ideas on handling
stresses within the family.*

National Stepfamily Association
Chapel House
3rd Floor
18 Hatton Place
London EC1N 8RU
0171-209-2460
*Local groups meet regularly to discuss
the problems which step-families
commonly face.*

Gingerbread
16-17 Clerkenwell Close
London EC2R 0AA
0171-336-8183
*Support group for single parents. Regular
meetings help parents air problems they
face raising children on their own.*